The Wish That Came True

A *Timeless Story*™
retold by Kumuda Reddy, M.D.
and John Emory Pruitt
illustrated by Chandu

Acknowledgments

I would like to thank my loving family, Dr. Susan Dillbeck, Stan and Marion Kendz, Cathy Ertelt, Cathy Cullerton, Laura Wysong, Linda Egenes, and William Groetzinger for their warm support and encouragement.

♥

Text and illustrations copyright © 1997 by Kumuda Reddy, M.D. All rights reserved.
Printed in Singapore

Color separations of original art by **Distinctive Color**, Colorado Springs USA
Layout and prepress production by William Groetzinger

Published by Timeless Stories
183 Saint Paul Street, Rochester, New York 14604
Phone: 1-800-784-2773

ISBN: 1-57582-051-X

Other **Timeless Stories** available soon:

The Female Mouse   *The Hares and the Elephants*

The Indigo Jackal   *The Lion and the Hare*

The Monkey and the Crocodile

This book is dedicated with love and gratitude to my parents,
Kameswaramma and Harischandra Reddy,
for their unbounded and unconditional love for their family,
friends, and everyone blessed to have known them.

Preface

It started in early 1992. During one of our visits to a local bookstore, my father, a very loving and enlightened man, mentioned that among the many storybooks for children, he didn't see many that taught children worldly wisdom, good values, or the practical matters of life. I immediately thought of the hundreds of wonderful traditional stories from my childhood in India. I remembered how much they had delighted and influenced me as I was growing up. My father was remembering them too.

My father recently passed away and the seeds he planted in my heart that day are now beginning to bear fruit. Storytelling is a timeless tradition in India. My grandmother was a master storyteller, just like my dad. During vacations and free time, we would gather around her and listen to these ageless stories. The grandchildren listening to her were of all ages, from one-year-old to college-age. It wasn't important how much we understood. We all listened in complete rapture, each at our own level. The tales she told were universal and had practical importance to both our lives and the whole cosmos. Some had a clear message, while others were more subtle.

These stories are centered around wisdom in life. Woven throughout the stories are principles that support the use of common sense and prudence.

We recommend simply reading or listening to them, enjoying them, and then forgetting them. These stories and their meanings will get stored in your memories. When the time is right, they will return as gentle reminders and aids in facing the myriad problems and mysteries in life. My own children, born and raised here in the United States, have heard and read many of these stories. They, too, have benefited from their wisdom and truly cherish this tradition.

It is my intent to make these stories available to all children. My wish is that children be nurtured through this subtle method of teaching, in preparation for life in the world. Children of all ages will enjoy these stories. Parents, grandparents, and teachers will find them entertaining.

Let us read these timeless tales with the intent of creating a better life for all children.

—Kumuda Reddy, M.D.

Introduction

These stories are not new. In fact, they are some of the oldest stories we know. They were written down over 2000 years ago, and they were probably first created long before that. When they first appeared in ancient times as a book, the collection of stories was called *Panchatantra* (pronounced pon-cha-**ton**-tra), which means five (pancha) books (tantra). They were written in Sanskrit, a very ancient language, the language of the Veda.

These stories are part of another story which goes like this: Once there was a king who had three sons. The king loved his sons, his country, and his people. He always tried his best to be a good king. He was so devoted that all he thought about was making people happy. He thought about them all the time. He even thought about the people in his kingdom who weren't born yet. He wondered how he could make sure they would be as happy and healthy as the people living then.

His three sons, however, did not think like their good father. They were completely silly and just wanted to play games and be pampered princes. They didn't learn a thing in school and had no concerns for their future. They did not care about what they would be doing when it came time for them to rule the country. This worried the king a lot. He thought about this day and night, and it made him very unhappy. How could he leave the problems of a whole country to his three sons, who didn't have a clue about the duties of rulership?

The king called a meeting of his advisors and told them about his problem. They argued and debated for a whole week about what to do with his lazy boys. But nobody came up with an idea that the king liked, until one young man in his court stood up and recommended that they consult his own teacher, Vishnu Sharma. This teacher was quite old and had a reputation for being a truly great and wise man. He was retired, but he came to the court at the king's request. After hearing the king's cry for help, Vishnu Sharma said that if he couldn't teach the king's three sons everything they needed to know about leadership, diplomacy, and all the duties lying ahead of them within six months' time, then he would not be worthy of his own name.

So off he went with the princes. In order to capture their attention, he devised stories to entertain and teach them at the same time. These stories were full of adventures, strange animals, and interesting people. He was a great storyteller, and the princes listened raptly as he instilled the wisdom of life into their hearts. In six months' time, the three princes learned all they needed to know to become fine rulers.

Vishnu Sharma took them back to the king and tested them before the whole court. Every question about diplomacy, leadership, commerce, defense, and government was thrown at the three young men and they answered each one with great wisdom, remembering the lessons that Vishnu Sharma had set down so perfectly in their hearts. The king was very happy and Vishnu Sharma was known from that day on as the greatest teacher of *nitishastra* (pronounced nee-tee-**sha**-stra), or the teachings of how to live life in accord with all the laws of nature.

The stories in this series are presented one at a time instead of being woven together, as was done in the original Panchatantra. There are so many stories that it will take many volumes to tell them all. They are the same stories that were told over 2,000 years ago, but they are told just for you, in a way that we hope is both fun and beneficial. It is our wish that you take into your hearts the wisdom and teachings of the ancient Vishnu Sharma, so that you too know how to live a life full of bliss, a life perfectly in accord with all the laws of nature.

The Wish That Came True

The mark of a great man is vision
And his dream of a much higher goal.
But the mark of a fool is his blindness—
Eyes fixed on his own begging bowl.

I n a little town near the seashore lived a cloth weaver named Budhu. He worked very hard at his trade, and one day while he was weaving, the wood beams on his loom broke. They had finally given out from old age and years of hard use. No more weaving could be done until they were repaired, so Budhu picked up his ax and went off to find some wood.

Wandering along the shore, he came upon a great old tree, whose wood was known for making the very best tools. Looking up into the wide canopy, the weaver imagined how many good things he could make from such a fine tree.

He picked up his keen-bladed ax and swung it into the tree. It landed on the bark with a loud "whack." As he pulled the ax out for the second blow, he heard a strange voice.

"Wait, please stop! This tree is my home!"

Budhu jumped in fright, dropping his ax. "Who is that?" he called, with trembling voice.

"It is me, Tree Heart. I am an old tree spirit, and this has been my home for seven hundred and thirty-one years. Please don't cut me down! I love living here next to the cool ocean breezes, and I love listening to the waves, the rain, and the birds. I want to stay here in this beautiful spot for at least another fifteen hundred and twenty-seven years. Then I will be happy to move someplace else."

Budhu was not sympathetic. He said rudely, "Well, that's nice, but I have a broken loom back home and a living to make. I need the excellent wood from this tree. So you can just move today instead of in fifteen hundred and twenty-seven years. So there."

With that, Budhu picked up his ax and wound up for another swipe at the tree's barky torso.

"Wait! Wait! Don't hit my trunk again, please! If you go away and leave me in peace, I will grant you anything you desire. That is my special power and my gift to you for sparing my home. That is why this tree is so old and healthy. I have granted a wish to a hundred ninety-seven axmen over the last seven hundred and thirty-one years. And if your wish does not get fulfilled exactly as you desire, then feel free to come back and chop my home to pieces."

"Any wish, you say? Any wish at all?" he asked. Budhu scratched his chin, trying to imagine what he might ask for, but not much happened inside his thick skull. He had just come out for some wood. Now suddenly it seemed he could have anything that he could imagine. It was more than his dull mind could ponder.

"Yes," the tree spirit called. "Any wish you can think of, however grand, will be yours. As soon as you say it here under my tree, along with the magic words *'by the power of my friend the tree spirit, so be it now and forever,'* then it's all yours."

"All right!" Budhu cried. "It's a deal! Can I go home and think about my wish for a while? This is surely the biggest decision of my life."

"Why, certainly, my friend. Take all the time you want. Come back whenever you are ready to make your wish come true."

With that, Budhu shouldered his ax and walked back to his village, scratching his head and trying to think of a good wish. When he got to town, he met his friend the barber. He and Budhu sat down under the tree where the barber cut hair and shaved the townsmen. Budhu told him the story of the tree spirit and how he had to come up with the best possible wish. He confessed how difficult this was for him, being slow-witted.

"Budhu, think of it!" said the barber, waving his razor about in the air. "You could be a king and have a whole country to rule. And I could be your chief minister. We could have everything any man ever dreamed of, just with one little wish. We could be wealthy, famous, well fed, and well dressed. We could be worshipped by the people, and we could have many wives, children, and grandchildren. Our lives could be soft and easy. We could be known around the world for generations! I think you should wish to be a king!"

Budhu's eyes lit up with excitement. "Well, that sounds brilliant, my friend. I never would have thought of that. In an instant, your imagination has taken us to the highest possibilities! A king! Me, Budhu the weaver, a real king! But, Barber, who would weave my cloth for me while I was busy kinging about?"

"Budhu!" cried the barber. "Nobody would have to weave your cloth. You would have more important things to do. Forget your stupid weaving, man. This is the time to dream! And as for me, your chief minister, I would never again pick up scissors or a razor for as long as I live!"

Budhu clapped his hands together and cried, "Well, it's done then! I'll go home and tell my wife. She will be so happy!"

"No, don't do that!" the barber warned. "These are important matters. She may come up with some foolish, practical wish that would ruin our plans. I say, don't tell her at all. Let her become queen as a surprise. Then we'll all be happy for the rest of our lives."

"Barber!" said Budhu, shocked at his advice. "I couldn't do that!

I have always depended on my wife to help me with decisions. I can't betray her now. She is a good woman. She will surely agree with our idea. Who could argue with living the greatest life imaginable? She will go for it. I know she will." With that, Budhu got up from his stool under the barber's shade tree and walked back to his little cottage. The barber shook his head in sadness and went back to shaving customers.

"Wife, I am home. Come quickly—I have good news," Budhu called as he ran into the cottage.

"Oh, really," his wife replied. "And where is the wood you went after to fix your loom?"

Budhu smiled and hugged his wife. "That's what I have to tell you, dear. There is a tree spirit living in the tree I chose to cut. He promised me any wish if I would leave his tree unharmed. And better yet, I just visited with my friend the barber. He came up with a plan! He advised me to wish to be a king! Imagine, me a king and you a queen! What a life we would have together!"

"Forget it!" she yelled. "Can you imagine all the work it would take to keep a palace? How could I ever keep it clean and tidy? I have plenty to do right here in this little cottage. What makes you think you are wise enough to rule a kingdom, anyway?

You can barely take care of your weaving. And why do you consult a lowly barber about your affairs? What does he know about being a king? He has only haircuts and whiskers to worry about. I think it's a terrible idea!"

Budhu started scratching his head again. He didn't know what to do now that his wife had trampled on the idea. His head hurt from trying to grasp her reasoning, as it often did when she advised him. "Well, I guess you have a point. What would you have me wish for, since you don't like my idea?"

"Something practical, something useful, something that won't make problems for me," she snapped at him. "How about this? Why don't you ask for another set of arms and another head? That way you could work two looms at once and weave twice as much cloth. With all that extra cloth we would have enough money to buy a few nice things around here. Then we could at last have an easier life. You could even help me with the cleaning with your extra hands and spare time."

"That's a brilliant idea!" he cried, clapping his hands together. "Imagine, twice as much cloth. We could buy more vegetables and some cheese now and then. Wouldn't that be nice?" So off went Budhu on the advice of his practical-thinking wife.

When he got to the tree, he called out to the resident tree spirit. "Yoo-hoo, tree spirit. I am back. Yoo-hoo!"

"Yes, yes, I hear you," the spirit said. "Weaver, have you decided on a wish yet?"

Budhu rubbed his hands together in excitement. "Yes, I have. Are you ready?"

"Let's have it, then," replied the tree spirit.

"All right. Here it is." Budhu blurted out, "I wish to have two extra arms and an extra head, so that I can do twice as much work at my loom."

The tree spirit chuckled to himself and said, "Now, don't forget the other part, Weaver, or it won't work."

"Oh, yes, of course." Budhu scratched his head trying to remember the whole thing at once. "I wish to have two extra arms and an extra head so that I can do twice as much work at my loom, *by the power of my friend the tree spirit, so be it now and forever.*" There was a sudden flash in the air, like a little lightning bolt followed by a big puff of blue smoke. When the smoke drifted away, there was Budhu. Two identical heads and two extra arms sprouted from his shoulders.

"You did it!" shouted Budhu, waving his four arms and dancing around under the tree.

"Please go home now, Weaver, and enjoy your wish," said the tree spirit. Budhu happily ran off to show his wife his new head and limbs. On the way he passed through the village. It was market day, and many people were bustling about. Budhu was so excited that he ran right into the crowd, shouting and waving his many arms about him. All of the people screamed in terror at the horrible man

with two heads. Thinking he was a demon who had come to kill
them, everyone ran to hide. The bravest men, though, ran and got
their swords and axes. They chased Budhu all around the village
market. They chased him right out of town and far away into the
far-off woods and mountains. They chased him where he could
never, ever find his way home again.

Then it was that Budhu got the notion into both his heads: how foolish he had been to take short-sighted advice. But it was too late. What was done could not be undone. Budhu had to live with his choice until the end of his days.

Wish what you wish but beware,
And wish with this great wisher's clue:
Wish with true wisdom and wish from your heart,
Or you'll wish that your wish never came true.

Kumuda Reddy, M.D.

Dr. Kumuda Reddy is a former faculty member and anesthesiologist at Albany Medical College. She is currently an adjunct faculty member and practices Maharishi Ayur-Veda natural health care with conventional medicine in Schenectady, New York. Dr. Reddy lives in Niskayuna, New York with her husband Janardhan, a practicing urologist, and her three children: Sundeep, Hima, and Suma. In addition to writing children's stories, Dr. Reddy writes and lectures on the Maharishi Ayur-Veda approach. Her most recent publication is *Forever Healthy: Introduction to Maharishi Ayur-Veda Health Care.*

Kumuda Reddy, M.D.
1537 Union Street
Schenectady, NY 12309

e-mail address: mavhc@aol.com

John Emory Pruitt

John is a teacher of the Transcendental Meditation program. He has a B.A. in art, writing, and education from the State University of New York and has studied additionally in Switzerland and India. John resides in Rochester, New York where he enjoys songwriting, fiddling, cooking, and sports.

Chandu

A. Chandrasekhar, known as Chandu, is a native of Orissa, India. He has been an illustrator for fifteen years and has published his work in several magazines. Chandu currently lives in Hyderabad, India with his wife Chandra and two daughters, Kirtana and Sruti.